Planet Earth

Contents

Julie Haydon

CROSBY
HEIGHTS
PUBLIC
SCHOOL

NELSON
THOMSON LEARNING™

Australia · Canada · Mexico · Singapore · Spain · United Kingdom · United States

Planet Earth

We live on the planet Earth.
Earth is round,
like a ball.

Earth has air and water,
and is warmed by the sun.

Earth is the only planet
we know of
where animals and plants live.

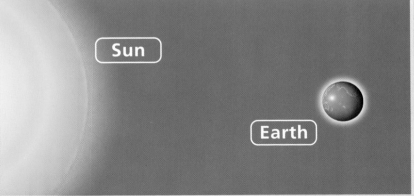

Sun

Earth

Inside Earth

Scientists think
there is a giant metal ball
at the centre of Earth.
This metal ball is called
Earth's core.

The rest of Earth is made of rock.
Some of this rock
is so hot,
it has melted.

This rock is so hot,
it has melted.

4

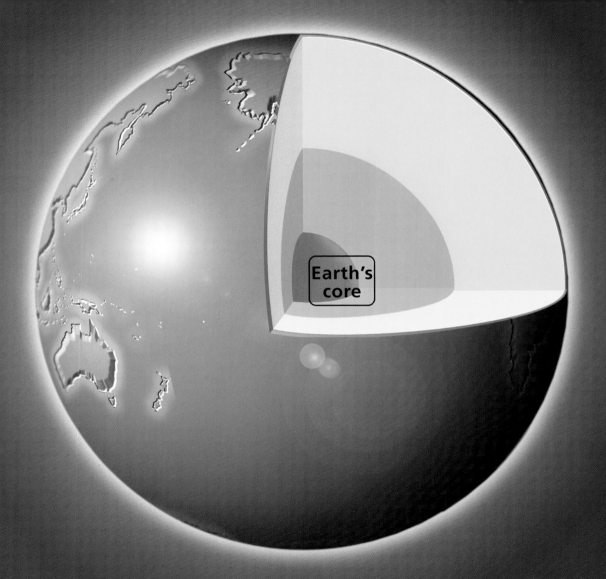

Earth's core

Earth's Crust

The surface of Earth is called **Earth's crust.**

Most of Earth's crust is covered by water.

Earth's crust is covered by land and water.

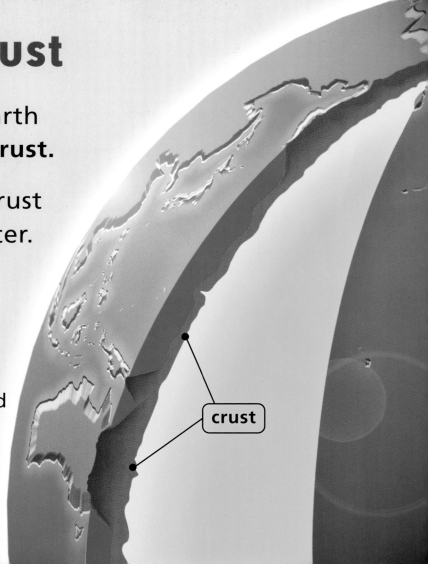

crust

The Blue Planet

Most of Earth is covered with water. From space, our planet looks blue!

The Oceans

Most of the water on Earth is salt water.
The salt water makes up Earth's oceans.

- Pacific Ocean
- Atlantic Ocean
- Indian Ocean
- Arctic Ocean
- Southern Ocean

Pacific Ocean

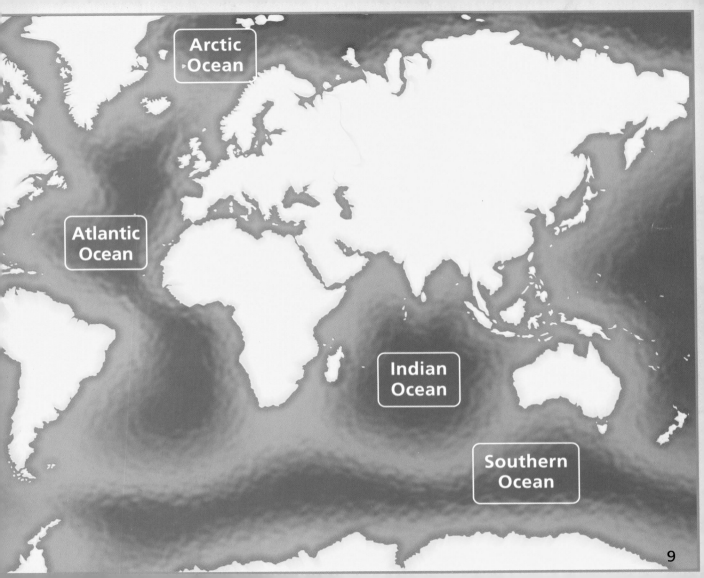

The Continents

Earth has seven main pieces of land called **continents**.

- Asia
- Africa
- North America
- South America
- Antarctica
- Europe
- Australia

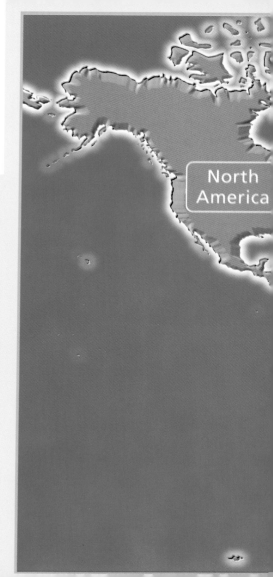

North America

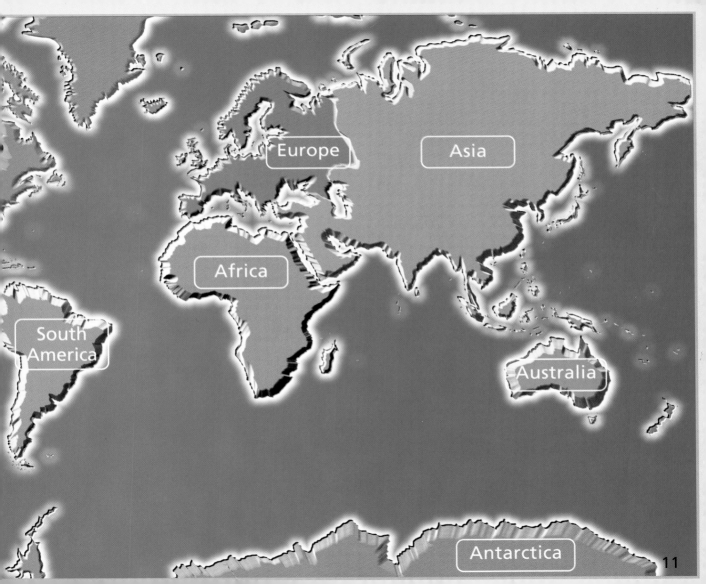

Parts of Earth

Parts of Earth look different.

Deserts get very little rain.
They have very few plants.

Deserts on Earth

Forests on Earth

Forests have lots of trees.
Forests get plenty of rain.

Mountains are made of rock.
A group of mountains
is called a mountain range.

Mountains on Earth

Ice and snow cover some parts
of Earth all year round.

Ice and snow on Earth

Glossary

continents   Earth's seven main pieces of land

Earth's core   the giant metal ball at the centre of Earth

Earth's crust   the surface of Earth. It is made of rock.

Index